Dear mouse friends,
Welcome to the world of

# Geronimo Stilton

THE RODENT'S GAZETTE
EDITORIAL STAFF

**Geronimo Stilton**
A learned and brainy
mouse; editor of
*The Rodent's Gazette*

**Thea Stilton**
Geronimo's sister and
special correspondent at
*The Rodent's Gazette*

**Trap Stilton**
An awful joker;
Geronimo's cousin and
owner of the store
Cheap Junk for Less

**Benjamin Stilton**
A sweet and loving
nine-year-old mouse;
Geronimo's favorite
nephew

# Geronimo Stilton

## THE STICKY SITUATION

Scholastic Inc.

Copyright © 2017 by Edizioni Piemme S.p.A., Palazzo Mondadori, Via Mondadori 1, 20090 Segrate, Italy. International Rights © Atlantyca S.p.A. English translation © 2020 by Atlantyca S.p.A.

The publisher does not have any control over and does not assume any responsibility for author or third-party websites or their content.

GERONIMO STILTON names, characters, and related indicia are copyright, trademark, and exclusive license of Atlantyca S.p.A. All rights reserved. The moral right of the author has been asserted. Based on an original idea by Elisabetta Dami. geronimostilton.com

Published by Scholastic Inc., *Publishers since 1920*, 557 Broadway, New York, NY 10012. SCHOLASTIC and associated logos are trademarks and/or registered trademarks of Scholastic Inc.

*Stilton is the name of a famous English cheese. It is a registered trademark of the Stilton Cheese Makers' Association.*

This book is a work of fiction. Names, characters, places, and incidents are either the product of the author's imagination or are used fictitiously, and any resemblance to actual persons, living or dead, business establishments, events, or locales is entirely coincidental.

ISBN 978-1-338-58756-2

Text by Geronimo Stilton
Original title *Te lo do io il miele, Stilton!*
Cover by Iacopo Bruno (art director), Andrea Da Rold, and Christian Aliprandi
Illustrations by Danilo Loizedda, Antonio Campo, and Daria Cerchi
Graphics by Marta Lorini

Special thanks to Anna Bloom
Translated by Anna Pizzelli
Interior design by Kay Petronio

10 9 8 7 6 5 4 3 2 1          20 21 22 23 24

Printed in the U.S.A.          40
First printing 2020

# Buzz, Buzz, Buzz!

Spring had officially sprung in **NEW MOUSE CITY**, the capital of Mouse Island. And it was **Friday**! So I was in a ratastic mood!

My name is Stilton, *Geronimo Stilton*, and I am the editor in chief of *The Rodent's Gazette*, the most famouse newspaper on Mouse Island.

What a mouserific day!

Finally, the weekend was here, and my vacation was starting. I couldn't wait to enjoy a well-deserved break. I'd been working my tail off! I left the office and walked to my bicycle, happily whistling a tune.

My backpack had everything I needed, including my **lucky** plaid shirt. It's the one I always wear when I spend time in the country! I was headed to the most mouserific place in the whole world, the Stilton family farm.

Ahhhh, the country . . . I love *Stilton Farm*. I got on my bike, singing:

There's nowhere with more charm,
Than the delightful Stilton Farm.
How I do love the country.
Life moves so slowly!
I can't wait to snack on cheeses,
While enjoying nice cool breezes.
Oh, Stilton Farm, how I love you,
Doo de doo, doo de doo!

I arrived in the afternoon and pedaled through the front gates up to the farmhouse's front door. Had there ever been a **lovelier** spot?

The sun gleamed bright above me and there wasn't a **cloud** in the sky. Birds chirped in the trees, chickens clucked outside the henhouse, and cows grazed in a nearby field. What a beautiful day!

Everymouse in the Stilton family is welcome to use the farm whenever they want. Tonight we were having a big party to

Finally!

celebrate the beginning of spring. I was looking forward to seeing all my favorite rodents — but also to enjoying a little peace and quiet before they arrived!

As I pedaled closer to the house, some horses galloped toward me. A donkey joined them, staring at me with his sweet eyes. I was so happy the animals recognized me!

I waved to all of them with my paw. "Hello, friends!" I slowed to a stop at the front door and dug through my backpack for my keys. Just as I was about to turn the doorknob, I felt a sharp PAIN in my tail!

"OUCHHHH!"

Ouchhhh!

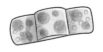

# SWEET SMELL OF SUCCESS?

I checked my tail (I'm very fond of my tail!), and I realized a bee had STUNG me. I threw open the door and ran inside, screaming, "SQUEAK!"

I closed the door, breathed a sigh of relief, and went to put a **bandage** on my tail. "Geronimo!" someone cried. Moldy mozzarella sticks! I was so surprised, I almost dropped my first-aid ointment.

It was my cousin Trap. "Are you hurt? Did a bee STING you?"

"What in the name of sliced Gouda are you doing here?" I cried.

Trap sighed. "Didn't you get my text?"

"I certainly did not," I said.

Trap looked down at his phone and chuckled. "Oh, I'm so **SILLY**. I accidently texted my friend Geraldo Stiltoney instead of you!"

What a **cheddarhead**!

But Trap just shrugged. "Oh well. My text was just to let you know to be careful because the farm has a lot of **bees** flying around right now."

I patted my **tender** tail. "Yeah, I guess I found that out the hard way."

"You can say that again, Geronimo!" Trap **enthusiastically** patted my back. A bit too **enthusiastically** . . . I pitched forward and almost fell on my snout.

"**CAREFUL**, Trap!" I said. "My tail is still sore!" I regained my balance and peered more closely at the sting. "What are you doing here early anyway? I had a nice quiet afternoon planned for myself."

"Nice and quiet is overrated!" Trap exclaimed. "I have been working on a special **SURPRISE** for you — and now, I'm finally ready to show you what it is!" Trap paused dramatically and wiggled his eyebrows at me.

I stared back at him.

"Go ahead, ask me what the **SURPRISE** is," Trap said eagerly.

I crossed my paws in front of my chest

and rolled my eyes. "Fine. Trap, what is your **SURPRISE**?"

Did I even want to know?

"Drumroll, please!" Trap started to play a pretend drum set with his paws. When I didn't join in, he stopped and darted over to the large living room closet.

He winked, a mischievous look on his snout. "Get ready to thank me, Geronimo. As of today, we will have a BRAND-NEW product available at the farm." He threw open the closet door and pulled out some sort of costume.

"What is that?" I asked.

"It's a beekeeper's suit, of course! We're going to have **honey** on the farm!"

My mouth dropped open.

"Don't worry. I have one for you, too!"

Trap cried, pulling a second suit out of the closet.

"I love eating honey, so I decided we should also make it! You can **bee** my assistant, Geronimo!" Trap danced over my way and handed me the second beekeeper suit. "**QUICK**, go change and I will show you around!"

I groaned but took the suit and went to

Before

After

This is me, Geronimo Stilton.

This is me, Geronimo Stilton, expert beekeeper! The suit lets me get close to the beehives without getting stung.

put it on. I would never hear the end of it if I didn't at least go take a look. I just hoped I wouldn't get stung again.

Squeak! My poor tail!

Trap rubbed his paws together. "Once we produce enough **all natural honey**, we can sell it in town. Maybe we can call it Stilton Farm's Famouse Honey!"

"Famouse?" I said. "No one knows about it yet."

"Don't be such a **worryrat**, Geronimo! Pretty soon, every rodent on Mouse Island will be lining up for our honey. Just you wait and see!"

I shook my snout. "I don't know about that, Trap."

But Trap didn't seem to hear me. His eyes **GLOWED**

with excitement, like two balls of fresh mozzarella. "Once the honey starts selling, we can take Stilton Farm to the next level and build a greenhouse. That way, we can grow vegetables all year round!"

I could see that Trap was getting carried away, but once he has an idea, there's usually no stopping him!

"Quick, go change your clothes! The bees wait for no mouse!" Trap cried, pushing me toward the bathroom. "Soon the SUN will be setting and the bees will be going to sleep. We don't want them to get anxious!"

**ANXIOUS** bees? What in the world was Trap going

I'm coming!

Hurry, let's go!

on about? Would **ANXIOUS** bees be more likely to sting me? **Squeak!** We better **SHAKE OUR TAILS** and get going! I rushed to change, and Trap told me all about bees.

Here are the beehives! This is where the bees make their honey!

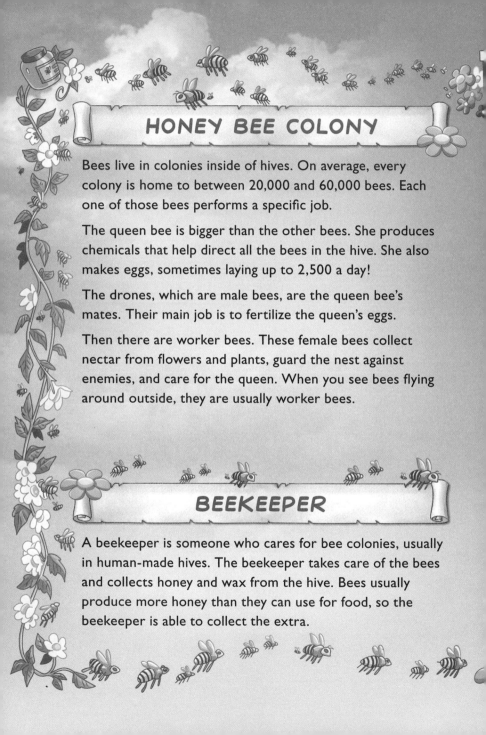

# HONEY BEE COLONY

Bees live in colonies inside of hives. On average, every colony is home to between 20,000 and 60,000 bees. Each one of those bees performs a specific job.

The queen bee is bigger than the other bees. She produces chemicals that help direct all the bees in the hive. She also makes eggs, sometimes laying up to 2,500 a day!

The drones, which are male bees, are the queen bee's mates. Their main job is to fertilize the queen's eggs.

Then there are worker bees. These female bees collect nectar from flowers and plants, guard the nest against enemies, and care for the queen. When you see bees flying around outside, they are usually worker bees.

# BEEKEEPER

A beekeeper is someone who cares for bee colonies, usually in human-made hives. The beekeeper takes care of the bees and collects honey and wax from the hive. Bees usually produce more honey than they can use for food, so the beekeeper is able to collect the extra.

# HONEY

Honey is the sticky, sweet substance produced by bees. They also use it as food.

Other animals also enjoy honey — like humans! The flavor of honey can vary depending on the kinds of plants and flowers that the bees have visited. That is how you get different varieties, like manuka honey. Honey can be used in a number of ways to sweeten everything from a cup of tea to a birthday cake!

# COLONY COLLAPSE DISORDER

Bees are a very important part of the ecosystem. As they travel around collecting nectar, they are helping to pollinate a wide number of trees, flowers, and other types of plants. Without the help of bees, many crops are unable to grow fruit and reproduce.

This is why farmers, beekeepers, and scientists are worried about a phenomenon called colony collapse disorder. This happens when an entire colony of bees dies off suddenly. No one is sure exactly what causes this, but scientists agree that it is probably related to a variety of factors, including pesticide use, climate change, loss of habitat, and infections caused by viruses, mites, or fungus.

# HIVE SWEET HIVE

Trap pointed to ten **brightly** colored wooden boxes, all in a line. "These are the **beehives**. This is where the bees make their honey."

I stepped forward to get a closer look and tripped over my own tail. The sudden movement must have upset the bees. They started **buzzing** more loudly and swirling around me.

"Stay calm!" Trap shouted. "Don't move any more, or you'll make things worse."

I stood up slowly and stayed perfectly still. The bees stopped *swirling* around me and headed back to their hives.

Stay calm!

Trap didn't seem to notice how **SCARED** I had been. He clapped his paws together. "Let's get to work. First, we'll make a list of everything you'll need to do."

This didn't sound good. But I got out some paper and a pencil.

"Item one," Trap said, "Geronimo will clear leaves and branches from the path to the beehives. Item two, Geronimo will **collect** honey from the hives." He ducked inside a wooden shack and waved for me to follow him. "Item three: Geronimo will fill these jars with honey and label them."

"**WAIT!**" I squeaked angrily. "Why do I have to do everything?"

Help!

Trap tripped and all the jars crashed to the floor.

I fell in a puddle of sticky honey . . .

And a bunch of leaves stuck to me!

Trap just laughed. "You actually have all the easy-squeezy jobs. I am the one who has been doing all the **bee** research and setting everything up!"

Trap turned toward the shack and lost his balance. He tripped and accidently pulled the tablecloth off the table, sending full jars of **honey** crashing to the ground.

He **whirled** around in an attempt to catch some of the jars and knocked into me. I went flying, paws over snout, and landed in a puddle of super-sticky **honey**. When I got up, I was covered from the tips of my ears to the tip of my tail!

Then the wind gusted, sticking leaves all over me.

**OH NO!**

I couldn't see anything ... but I could hear a loud *BUZZING* sound getting closer and closer.

*BUZZ BUZZ BUZZ*

The bees were getting anxious again!

I staggered out of the honey shack and tried to peel the leaves off my snout. But — **SMASH!** — my paw hit the corner of

I knocked over the roof of a beehive ...

... and all the bees got out!

A swarm of bees started chasing me!

one of the beehives! CRASH! The roof flew off and more bees zoomed out to see what was going on. They swarmed around me, attracted by the smell of all the honey stuck in my fur.

Behind me, Trap ran out of the honey shack. I thought he would distract the bees. But he just kept running!

"I'm getting out of here, Geronimo!" he shouted.

Rancid ricotta! I started running, too!

Before I knew it, I had reached the edge of the farm. There was Stilton Pond! I picked up speed and launched myself into the pond with an ENORMOUSE splash.

I held my breath underwater for as long as I could possibly stand it. When I finally poked my snout back out above the water, the bees were gone. I was safe!

# BEE MINE

As soon as I got out of the pond, I started walking back toward Stilton Farm. The sun was SETTING and it was getting COLDER. I started to walk faster, but then I noticed something strange out of the corner of my eye.

A TALL concrete cube rose up into the sky. Workers in construction hats scrambled

What's that?

around, and tall cranes lifted equipment up to the roof.

My **snout** dropped open in awe. What in the name of shredded cheddar was this *MYSTERIMOUSE* new building?

Some of the workers were attaching an **ENORMOUSE** sign to the front of the building. I crept forward, trying to figure out what it said.

A long line of black-and-yellow trucks came in and out of the strange building.

Were they picking something up? Dropping it off? The workers finally finished the sign and I got a good look at it:

Trap won't be happy about this! We had competition now — big competition, by the looks of that building! But where were the bees going to make the **honey**? It didn't seem like they had any trees, flowers, or wildlife around to support a massive **honey** production like that.

I was on my way back to Stilton Farm when another building caught my eye.

Unlike the **honey** factory, this building was TINY and surrounded by *beautiful* white flowers. It looked like something out of a *fairy tale* ... How fabumouse! I wondered who lived inside.

The sign out front said GOLDENDROP LODGE, ORGANIC MANUKA HONEY FOR SALE.

"**Manuka**," I said out loud. I didn't know what that word meant, but I wanted to find out!

A little old lady-mouse

came through the yard. She set down the flowers she had been carrying and waved a paw in my direction. "Hello, dear," she called. "Is everything okay? Do you need help?"

I suddenly realized I looked like a MESS! My beekeeper suit was torn and covered in mud. The bees had stung me everywhere, leaving huge welts! Crusty cheese niblets, no wonder she sounded concerned!

Yikes!

"Oh, no, thank you," I said sheepishly. "It looks worse than it is." I turned to go, but the rodent wouldn't take no for an answer.

"Come with me!" she called. "I have just the thing for those

**bee** stings!" I shrugged and followed her into the house.

In her kitchen, she examined my injuries. "You're in good paws," she assured me. "My name is Melanie Goldendrop, and I am a bee expert!"

# A Sweet Story

A **bee** expert! How marvemouse! I had a million questions, but before I could squeak, the door opened and another older rodent came in.

"This is my husband, Alpine," she said. "I'm sorry, but I didn't get your name yet."

Alpine just smiled. "No introductions needed! This is the **famouse** Geronimo Stilton, BIG CHEESE at *The Rodent's Gazette*!" He grabbed my paw and shook it up and down. "Pleased to have you in my home!" he said.

Alpine Goldendrop

I blushed, my fur turning ROSY.

"But enough chitchat," Alpine continued. "You're SOAKING wet! Let me lend you some dry clothes."

He opened a nearby closet and pulled out some things for me to wear.

After I changed clothes, we sat down to drink sage and peppermint herbal tea,

Here we go!

I love the Gazette!

sweetened with **honey**. Melanie had also set out a tray of warm cheddar biscuits. My favorite!

In between bites of biscuit, I asked Melanie and Alpine about the **sign** out front. "What exactly is **manuka** honey and what makes it different from other honey?"

"**Manuka** is a plant that grows in New Zealand and Australia," Melanie explained. "We grow the plant here to make and sell our own **manuka** honey to local rodents. It's what I used in the tea. Try some on the biscuits. It's so good! And it's good for you."

Then Alpine and Melanie told me all about how they got started in the **honey** business.

# Alpine and Melanie Goldendrop's Story

When we got married many years ago, we were young and adventurous ... and we loved **wildlife** and nature.

We decided that we would to go New Zealand on our **honeymoon**, because the countryside is so marvemouse. We slept outside in a tent, and in the mornings we would watch the sun rise behind beautiful wooded hills.

One day, while we were walking on a trail in the woods, we saw an incredimouse field of beautiful flowers. It looked just like **snow** and smelled deliciously sweet. Not far from there was a farm where they produced a **delightful honey**. The owner of the farm told us that the flowers we had seen were called **manuka**, and he used them to produce a very special kind of **honey**.

We ended up spending a whole year in New Zealand, studying bees and learning about **honey** production. When we returned to Mouse Island, we built this little house. We decided to plant the **manuka flowers** as a symbol of our love. We've been living here ever since, making **honey** with the same passion and joy as the very first time we tasted it!

"What a great story!" I exclaimed when they finished. "You know, we are actually just starting to make **honey** over at Stilton Farm," I said.

I could see them glance at my **bee** stings and exchange a look.

"You must let us help you," Melanie said. I shook my snout, but Alpine insisted.

"We got help all those years ago, and we'd love to pass it on," he said. "Let's start now!" He leaped to his **paws** and began to enthusiastically describe all the different types of **honey**.

Squeak! I hope I'm not in over my snout!

# TYPES OF HONEY

**ACACIA HONEY:** light color, with a mild flavor and flowery fragrance

**ORANGE BLOSSOM HONEY:** light golden, with a hint of citrus

**CLOVER HONEY:** amber colored, mild flavor

**ALFALFA HONEY:** light colored, mild flavor

**HEATHER HONEY:** reddish-orange color, with an earthy aroma

**EUCALYPTUS HONEY:** light colored, strongly flavored, with a medicinal scent

**SUNFLOWER HONEY:** yellow to golden in color, with a mild flavor

**MANUKA HONEY:** dark colored, with a slightly bitter flavor

**BLUEBERRY HONEY:** light amber, blueberry aftertaste

**DANDELION HONEY:** dark amber, tangy flavor

**LINDEN HONEY:** light color, strong aroma

# ROYAL BEES

After tea, my two new friends drove me back to Stilton Farm in their van. By the time we got there it was already **EVENING**. As we pulled in, I insisted that Alpine and Melanie stay for dinner.

"We'd LOVE to!" Melanie said.

While I had been gone, the rest of the Stilton family vacation party had all arrived. My nephew Benjamin and my niece Trappy were there; my sister, Thea; my aunt Sweetfur; and my grandfather William! Some of my other friends had arrived, too!

A fire roared in the fireplace, and Trap stood at the stove stirring his famous creamy *cheese polenta* (yum!). Alpine and Melanie helped me put dishes of food on the table as I explained to Trap how they were going to help us with our beekeeping.

All of a sudden, Melanie and her husband were quiet as mice. I felt my fur go cold. Holey cheese, had they changed their minds?

Alpine cleared his throat. "We're getting older, and caring for our bees has gotten more difficult. We are ready to take a break. So . . . we'd like to give you our HIVES and manuka plants so that you can keep the tradition going."

I gasped. "That's incredimouse!" I cried. "Thank you so much."

"Whoopee!" Trap hollered. We both hugged Alpine and Melanie.

"We're going to teach you everything we know," Melanie said. "You'll be making the best honey on Mouse Island in no time at all!"

The next morning, Melanie and Alpine brought over their beehives. They showed us the best places to put the hives and helped us plant new trees so that the bees could produce different types of honey. Finally, they brought the manuka plants and we planted them together.

Melanie grabbed my paw. "We're so excited to think that after all these years, the manuka seeds we brought with us are still bearing fruit . . . and they will continue to do so in the future, for many more generations of rodents!"

"Take good care of our bees!" Alpine said.

I put my paw over my heart. "We will treat them like royalty, cross my heart!"

Next to me, Creepella sighed dreamily.

"What a romantic story they have," she said. Her gaze swept over all the work we had just done. "This would be the most beautiful spot for someone to get married. You could have a white manuka flower bouquet and a cheddar cake with honey-flavored icing." She grinned at me.

**SQUEAK!**

I got out of there as quickly as I could. "Sorry, Creepella, I have to go! I have a lot of cheese on my plate right now. The bees need me!" I jogged away as fast as my paws could carry me!

# HOW TO REPLANT A SEEDLING

## 1. PICK THE RIGHT DAY AND TIME.

Choose a time of day that's not too hot or sunny, like early morning.

## 2. DIG A HOLE.

Make a hole in the soil for your seedling. The hole should be twice as wide as the root ball.

## 3. REMOVE YOUR SEEDLING FROM ITS POT.

Carefully take your seedling out of its pot and gently loosen the root ball.

## 4. PLANT THE SEEDLING.

Place your seedling in the ground and loosely fill in the hole with dirt.

## 5. WATER YOUR PLANT.

Gently pour water over your seedling. Enjoy watching your plant grow!

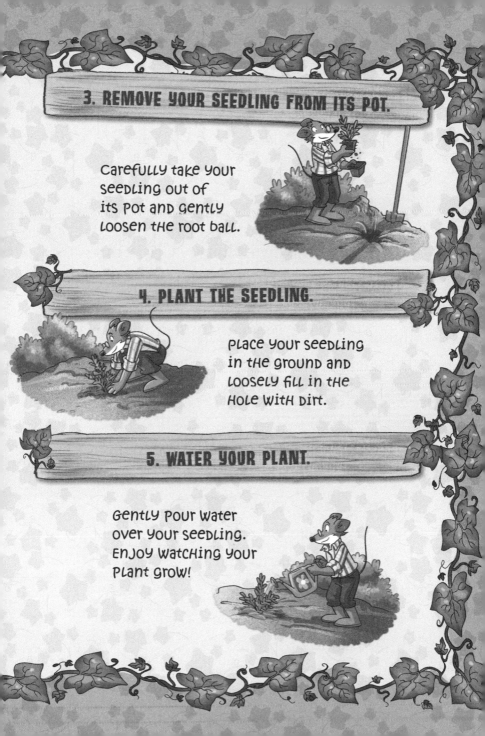

# A STICKY SITUATION?

After the weekend, my family and friends returned to New Mouse City. But my vacation was just getting started! With Trap's big plans for a **honey** business underway, my holiday was less relaxing than I thought it would be — but also even more fun. I actually really loved taking care of the bees!

Melanie and Alpine came by regularly to help Trap and me with the **HIVES**. Soon enough, our new **bees** had produced enough **honey** for us to start filling up jars we could sell. We couldn't wait for other rodents to taste it!

## What a sweet start!
## How exciting!

In the meantime, **Bee Mine** was becoming more and more **popular** on Mouse Island. The mysterimouse company had advertisements everywhere. I couldn't turn on the TV or radio without hearing about their **honey**. Then bus ads started cropping up. I was even getting emails about it. Rodents were buying bottles of it!

This was turning into a real **sticky situation**. Who would buy our honey if all they ever heard about was **Bee Mine**?

How could one honey company spend so much **MONEY** on advertising? When I first started seeing the TV ads, I suggested to Alpine and Melanie that we should buy some of our own. But they just shook their snouts.

# Bee Mine ADVERTISING

TV ADVERTISING

RADIO ADVERTISING

BUS ADVERTISING

NEWSPAPER ADVERTISING

EMAIL ADVERTISING

STREET POSTERS

"Good honey doesn't need FLASHY advertising," Alpine said. "Just concentrate on creating the best possible product, and the honey will sell itself!"

Trap and I had our doubts, but Melanie had assured me that word of snout was all we needed. "You'll see that once we take your honey to the SWEET TASTE OF MOUSE ISLAND honey competition, you won't be able to keep up with the demand!"

I hoped she was right. With their help, we were preparing for Mouse Island's most famous honey contest and planning visits to all the big NEW MOUSE CITY supermarkets to pitch our honey. If stores liked it, they would sell it to their customers!

All our friends helped out. Bruce Hyena volunteered to drive our honey around

New Mouse City. Thea took on the job of convincing store managers to give us a chance on their shelves. Trap

It's really good honey.

BAKED up a storm, creating new recipes that featured our delicious **honey**.

Surely, after all this work, rodents would stop buying so much Bee Mine and start picking up Stilton Farm instead!

Trust me!

# Honey Bee Cookie Recipe

Make buzz-worthy bee cookies! Always get a grown-up to help you!

INGREDIENTS: 2 ½ cups flour, 7 tablespoons butter, ¼ cup honey, ½ cup sugar, one egg, zest of one lemon, 5 to 10 drops yellow food coloring, almond slices, black decorating gel or icing

1. Mix the flour, butter, honey, sugar, egg, lemon zest, and food coloring in a bowl. Then shape the dough into a ball. Wrap the dough in plastic wrap and let it rest in the refrigerator for one hour.

2. Preheat your oven to 350 degrees. Line a baking sheet with parchment paper.

3. Scoop out a tablespoon of dough, roll it into a ball, and place it on the baking sheet. This is your bee's body. Place two almond slices into the ball. These are your bee's wings. Repeat until all the dough has been used. Bake for 10 to 15 minutes.

4. Once the cookies have cooled, use decorating gel or icing to give your bees stripes and eyes. Now enjoy your bee-utiful creations!

# YOU NEED
# TUMMYFIX!

Stilton Farm honey was getting more and more popular! Slowly, word of snout did seem to be helping to build sales. Trap and I felt ready for the **SWEET TASTE OF MOUSE**

ISLAND honey competition and were excited to have our special **manuka** honey judged by a team of expert rodents.

But it was hard to be happy about our progress because something STRANGE was happening around town . . . All of a sudden, many Mouse Island residents were complaining about Stomachaches.

# HMM...
# WHAT WAS GOING ON?

And even though our honey was becoming more and more popular, Bee Mine was still very popular. Rodents across the city seemed to be eating it for BREAKFAST, LUNCH, and **dinner**.

On my way back from pitching Stilton Farm Honey to a gourmet food store, I heard a truck go by, playing a familiar jingle:

"Tummy troubles? Don't get sad, get TummyFix!"

TummyFix? Where had I heard that before . . . Suddenly, I realized TummyFix was everywhere — on the truck, on the pharmacy window, on billboards.

I darted into the pharmacy and pushed my way to the front of the line. "Excuse me," I asked, ignoring the line of GRUMPY rodents behind me. "What is this TummyFix I've heard so much about?"

The pharmacist explained that it was a new, SUPER-EFFECTIVE medicine for stomach trouble. "Everymouse here is waiting for the next delivery," he explained.

I thanked him and stepped back outside. I rubbed my SNOUT in confusion. Maybe there was some sort of very contagious stomach flu going around?

This sure seemed like something I should look into for a *Rodent's Gazette* article. I was technically still on vacation, but this could be a cat-astrophe in the making! The news waits for no mouse.

I hopped on my bike and headed back to Stilton Farm. As soon as Trap and I were finished preparing for the **SWEET TASTE OF MOUSE ISLAND**, I would look into the STOMACH problems that seemed to be affecting everyone in the city.

But, for now, I had a trophy to win!

The following day, Bruce Hyena, Alpine, and Melanie helped Trap and me load up our van with Stilton Farm Honey. In addition to having our **honey** judged, we had the opportunity to sell it to the crowds of rodents attending the festival.

"This could be our big break, Geronimo!" Trap cried, hopping in next to Bruce.

"I hope so," I said, buckling my seatbelt. I

couldn't help myself, I was excited!

Behind us, Alpine and Melanie climbed into their car. They were going to follow us to the festival and help cheer us on. I couldn't wait to get there!

# AND THE
# WINNER IS . . .

When we got to the contest location, all the judges were getting ready to taste the different types of **honey**.

We added ours to the table, making sure to cover the Stilton Farm label. The jars all had to be disguised so that the judges wouldn't know whose **honey** was whose.

"Paws crossed," I whispered to Trap. We watched as the judges started to taste all the participants' honey.

"Hmm. This is GOOD . . ."

"But this one is better, don't you think?"

"This one is not very **sweet**."

"This one might be my favorite!"

**"YUCK."**

As the judges tasted everymouse's honey, Trap and I set up a small table to sell our jars. We worked our tails off, but holey cheese, it was going well!

We had just sold our last jar when we saw the judges rise to make an announcement.

"We're ready to declare a winner!" the head judge said. "The winning **honey** was unlike anything we've ever tasted! It is truly fabumouse! The winner is . . ." The judge peeled off the sticker covering the label. "Stilton Farm!"

## THUNDERING CATTAILS! WE DID IT!

Trap and I cheered. Everyone **clapped** for us as we walked up to claim our prize.

"Thank you so much for selecting Stilton Farm! I would like to accept this prize on behalf of the whole Stilton family," I said. All the rodents in the audience clapped again and a grin spread across my snout. "I'd also like to give a big thank-you to Melanie and Alpine Goldendrop, FABUMOUSE beekeepers, for teaching Trap and me

everything we needed to know about **honey**!"

As I stepped away with our award, a judge pulled me aside. He shook my paw. "Really **marvemouse** honey, Stilton! You could taste the **love** and care you put into it." I **blushed**. "Not like that Bee Mine," the judge continued. "I have no idea why it's been so popular recently!" He shook his **snout** and headed back to his fellow judges.

Just then, I felt something brush my side. I whirled around, but there was no one there. Instead, there was a note sticking out of my **POCKET**!

DEAR MR. GERONIMO STILTON,
INTERESTED IN SELLING YOUR FARM?
WE CAN MAKE YOU AN OFFER YOU
CAN'T REFUSE. PLEASE CONTACT
MYSTERIMOUSEBUYER@MOUSEISLAND.COM
FOR MORE INFORMATION.

Great GLISTENING gobs of mozzarella! I'd never sell the farm!

# TO BEE OR
# NOT TO BEE?

The following day, I set out for a bike ride. There's nothing I like better than a ride around Stilton Farm in the **fresh** morning air! I hadn't gotten very far when I heard a strange *BUZZING* sound coming from behind me. It sounded almost like **bees** . . . but no bees I'd ever heard before. I turned around

to see what was making the noise — and all my fur stood on end!

Sweltering Swiss cheese! A large swarm of bees hovered just above the ground. They shimmered strangely in the sunlight, almost like they were glowing.

Even the buzzing sound they made was different from normal bees: It was high-pitched and tinny.

**BUZZZZZ!**
**BUZZZZZ!**
**BUZZZZZ!**

Help!

The **cloud** of bees rose up in the air and started to move toward me. **RANCID RICOTTA!** I turned back around and pedaled faster. But every time I glanced over my shoulder, the bees were getting closer. They were definitely chasing me!

Just when it seemed like they might actually catch me, I heard a **beeping** sound. The **bees** immediately stopped in midair, turned around, and flew back the way they had come.

I *FLOPPED* over my handlebars, tired and sweating like a slice of cheese left out in the sun. Before I could catch my breath, I heard a car *roll* to a stop on the road.

When I looked up, a very long, **LEOPARD**-print car with dark tinted windows was idling in front of me. A back window slid down and a pointy snout appeared. The rodent inside wore dark **glasses**, but she looked strangely familiar.

Madame No is the CEO of EGO Corp. (Enormously Gigantic Organization), a powerful company that handles a lot of deals on Mouse Island. It develops shopping malls and skyscrapers, and it owns airline companies, newspapers, and TV stations. You don't say no to Madame No.

"Good morning, Stilton," she called.

I'd recognize that voice anywhere! It was Madame No!

"I'll get right to it," Madame No continued. "I have an offer for you. I would like to buy your *LITTLE* farm. I'll take everything as is — including your **beehives**. Just name your price."

I **twisted** my tail in my paws. "I love Stilton Farm and so do all my friends and family." I said. "I couldn't possibly — "

"Are you saying no to me?" Madame No interrupted.

"Yes! I mean, no! I'm not interested in selling!" I said.

"Fine. But you'll regret saying **NO** to Madame No, Stilton." She pressed a button inside the car and the window slid back up.

"YOU'LL REGRET THIS, STILTON!"

I **shivered**. What did she mean by that? And what did she want with *Stilton Farm*, anyway? This isn't the first time she's tried to buy it from me.

Madame No's car slowly drove away, then picked up speed and disappeared behind the first bend in the road, leaving me deep in thought.

If Madame No was lurking around, there was definitely something **rotten** going on. This whole situation STUNK like old cream cheese. I pedaled my way back to the farm and thought about all the odd things that had been going on recently.

It had all started with Stilton Farm's new neighbor, the Bee Mine factory.

Then there had been a stomach flu **outbreak** in New Mouse City.

Then there were those **metallic** bees.

And then the appearance of **MADAME NO** herself, and her request to buy Stilton Farm. I had to get to the bottom of these mysteries — and *FAST*!

Strange!
Very strange!

# TRAPPED LIKE A RAT!

The day after my odd meeting with Madame No, things at *Stilton Farm* got even stranger. Trap left for the day to take care of some errands in the city. When he was gone, I made myself a cheddar milkshake and decided to head outside to the hammock. My **VACATION** was almost over — I needed to relax a little!

But I didn't get very far. As soon as I poked my snout out the front door, the strange *BUZZING* sound from the day before started up again and a swarm of metallic bees charged the front door!

Couldn't a rodent catch a break?!

*BUZZZZZZZZZ!*

I tried to open the back **DOOR**, thinking I

BuzzZZZZZZZZZ Buzz
Buzz
Buzz

would be able to
get away without
them seeing me.
But there were bees waiting
for me there, too! They had
me surrounded!

Enough!

"Enough!" I squeaked. I'd
seen enough bees to last a lifetime. "Go away
and leave me **alone**!" I slumped down
against the door and put my SNOUT in
my paws.

As I sat, I heard more *BUZZING*. But
this time it didn't sound like bees. I stood
up and looked out the window. A small
drone hovered above the ground next to the

SWARM of metallic bees. As I watched, a voice boomed out of the drone's speaker: "Have you had enough, Stilton? I can take care of your little bee infestation problem, but first you have to agree to sell me the farm!"

MADAME NO AGAIN! How had Madame No heard about my bee problem? I could use the help, but there was no way I was going to sell the farm to get it! She'd gone too far!

"No way, Madame No!" I yelled through the window. "This farm is mine and I'm not selling!"

"I really think you should reconsider my offer while you can," Madame No called through the drone.

"Absolutely not!" I **YELLED**. Then I gathered up all my courage. "My family and

I love this farm and we're not letting it go! Now please *BUZZ OFF*!" I added.

The sound of chuckling came through the drone. "Very well, Stilton. I'll leave you to your bees," she hissed. "Good luck with your problem." The drone rose up high in the sky and disappeared over the house. Relief washed over me. I had gotten rid of Madame No, at least.

But it was short-lived. The *BUZZING* outside had gotten louder. Almost as if it was coming from inside the house . . .

**Moldy mozzarella! It was coming from inside the house!**

*HUNDREDS* of angry buzzing bees came streaming out of the fireplace and into my living room.

They must have found a way through the chimney! How did they get so smart? I ran out of the room and SLAMMED the door behind me, hoping to **TRAP** them inside.

I wedged a chair against the door to make sure it would stay closed and raced to find

my MousePhone. This bee problem had gotten out of control, and I needed all paws on deck. The first rodent I called answered the phone right away.

"Hercule Poirat, at your service," he said.

Who better to help me solve the **mystery** of the metallic bees than New Mouse City's finest rodent detective?

I explained all the **STRANGE** things that had been happening at the farm, as well as Madame No's recent threats. "And to make matters worse, I have a bee infestation!" I added. "I'm **TRaPPeD** in here! Please hurry!"

"You've called the right rodent, Geronimo! I will come as soon as I figure out what disguise will best fool the bees . . ."

"There's no time for that!" I squeaked. "Just come!" I hung up the **PHONE**.

The living room door rattled with the weight of the bees pressing against it. I could still hear their angry buzzing.

**GULP.**

# BEECOPTER

I stood still by the **WINDOW**, waiting for Hercule, until I finally heard a strange sound.

FLAP, FLAP, FLAP!

A large black-and-yellow shape came into view. It was a helicopter! The tail had been painted with stripes so that it looked like a bee. It wasn't just any old helicopter — it was a **beecopter**! The beecopter landed in a nearby field, and a rodent jumped out. As the rodent got closer, I could see that it was Hercule!

"Hercule!" I called though the window. "What are you wearing?"

Hercule hopped onto my front stoop and did a *twirl*. "I'm undercover!" Hercule exclaimed. "As a bee!" he continued, when I still looked **confused**.

And so he was. The puffy suit he wore had **BLACK**-and-**YELLOW** stripes, small **WiNGS**, and even a realistic **STINGER**!

"Let me in, Stilton, and let's get to work on your bee problem!" Hercule shouted.

"**SHHHHH!**" I hissed. "I don't want them to hear you."

"Who, the bees?" Hercule asked. "I think

all that honey you've been eating has gone to your head!"

I unlocked the front door and let Hercule inside. Anything to get him to be **QUIET**!

"Don't worry, Geronimo, I have a bee suit for you, too!" Hercule said. He hoisted the suitcase he'd brought with him onto a nearby chair. He unzipped it and pulled out a FOAM bee suit that was identical to the one he was wearing.

I poked it with my PAW. "But if we look like bees, won't the bees want to follow us more?" My whiskers quivered.

"It will be exactly the opposite, my dear Stilton!" Hercule assured me. "Bees don't bother other bees! And besides, the padding is so thick, we'll be protected from any stings."

I poked the suit again. It did seem to be pretty safe.

Hercule explained his plan to me while I got dressed. After we had our protective bee suits on, we'd release the metallic bees from my living room. Then we'd take the beecopter and follow them back to wherever they'd come from.

I am afraid of heights, but getting a bee's-eye view of the farm in Hercule's copter did sound like a good idea . . .

"You won't fly too high, right?" I asked.

"Sure, sure," Hercule said. "Don't be a worryrat. Once you feel the wind in your

How do I look?

Bee-utiful!

antennae, you'll totally forget how **HIGH** off the ground we are."

**SQUEAK!**

"Let's release the bees!" Hercule said, wiggling his antennae. "Ready?" he asked, approaching the living room door.

"Ready as I'll ever be, I guess," I said.

Hercule pushed the door wide open. "Start *BUZZING* like a bee!" he yelled. "And head for the copter!"

I buzzed and shook my STINGER as I sprinted for the beecopter. Hercule jogged beside me. A few of the STRANGE bees tried to sting us, but they quickly lost interest and started to fly away.

Hercule and I jumped into the beecopter and he started the engine.

"Hold on to your fur, Stilton!" Hercule yelled, and we ZOOMED into the air.

# THEY'RE BEEBOTS!

We flew over Stilton Farm's fields. The swarm in front of us ZIGGED and *zagged* around trees and fences, and Hercule ZIGGED and *zagged* the beecopter, too. I felt my stomach do flips.

"Be careful, Hercule," I said.

"Don't worry. You're in good paws," Hercule said. "We have to act like a bee to keep them from getting suspicious."

I clutched my stomach as Hercule swooped up high and then down low again. "Look," he said. "The bees are going into that square building over there."

I squinted into the distance and gasped. "That's the **Bee Mine** factory!" But what was next to it . . . a smaller building I hadn't

noticed before. The sign out front said
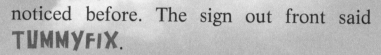TUMMYFIX.

Hercule slowed the **beecopter** and landed it behind a dumpster between the Bee Mine factory and the TummyFix factory.

I had never been so happy to be back on solid ground. When I looked up, Hercule was standing inside one of the dumpsters.

"What are you doing?" I hissed.

Hercule jumped out of the dumpster and held up a slightly **squashed** box. The label on the outside said *Beetronics Synthetic Wings*.

"I don't understand," I whispered, taking it. As Hercule passed it to me, an instruction manual fell out: *A Troubleshooting Guide to Your Robotic Bees*.

"Those metallic bees aren't bees at all!" Hercule said. "They're **ROBOTS**! And we're going to get to the bottom of what's really happening at these two factories." He held

up an empty box of TummyFix medicine he'd found in the same dumpster.

Together, we hid behind a stack of crates. As we waited, a large **BLACK**-and-YELLOW truck pulled up outside the factory.

A driver got out of the truck and pressed the intercom. "Truck number thirty-nine here!" he called.

A loud GRINDING noise followed and the gate at the entrance began to roll up. This was our chance! Hercule and I crept closer and closer. As we neared the open truck bay, the strange metallic *BUZZING* sound of the ROBOTIC BEES could be heard.

The angry voice of the truck driver also drifted out: "What do you mean the boxes aren't ready yet? I have a lot of deliveries to make! Can't these BEEBOTS work any faster?"

"**BEEBOTS!**" Hercule and I repeated, sharing a glance. We poked our snouts around the doorframe. Double twisted rat tails on toast! What we saw inside made our fur stand up on end.

Inside the factory there were **NO** bees, **NO** flowers, **NO** trees, and **NO** wooden beehives. Nothing resembling any of the honey-making supplies we had over at Stilton Farm.

Instead, the Bee Mine factory had only one giant metal **beehive**. Around it, thousands of **BEEBOTS** swarmed. They looked exactly like the ones that had been harassing me. Except here there were many more of them.

By the hive there was a sign that said

## HONEY MACHINE 5000
### Property of Professor No

To the left of the Honey Machine 5000 were containers marked honey fragrance, honey color, thickening agent, and honey flavoring.

The **BEEBOTS** worked diligently, adding different ingredients to the metal hive and mixing them together in **BIG** steel **honeycombs**. At the base of the machine, a golden liquid was piped into honey jars and sent down an assembly line to be labeled.

"The honey coming out of this factory is not made by real bees," I whispered. "It's not even real honey, it's some kind of **sticky** liquid that looks and smells like honey and is fooling everyone!"

"And then selling it to unsuspecting rodents all over Mouse Island," Hercule said, **frowning**.

A gray-haired rodent with a mean look

on his snout stalked around the machine, squeaking orders. He wore a crisp white lab coat and clutched a remote control.

# PROFESSOR NO!

Just then, we heard the sound of another vehicle approaching the factory. Hercule and I crept back behind the dumpsters and waited to see who it was.

"Let me in, you cheddarheads! It is I, Madame No!" She **jammed** her paw on the intercom button over and over until we heard the gate open and saw her car zoom into view.

I clutched my tail nervously. "Now what do we do?" I cried.

Professor No is Madame No's cousin. He is a ruthless inventor. He designs and manufactures robots and gadgets for Madame No to use.

# LET'S BEE FRIENDS!

While we were deciding what we should do next, Hercule noticed a **REMOTE CONTROL** with a broken antenna lying among the empty boxes. It looked just like the one **PROFESSOR NO** had been holding. A **Beetronics remote**! The remote had a lot of buttons that controlled various parts of the honey-making process. But the last button made my snout go cold.

"Beebot Attack: Geronimo Stilton," I read.

But Hercule didn't seem to notice my **alarm**. He had pulled a tiny set of tools out from

ADD DYE

ADD FRAGRANCE

ADD THICKENING AGENT

ADD FLAVOR

MIX WELL

BEEBOT ATTACK: GERONIMO STILTON

somewhere inside his bee suit and was tinkering with the remote.

FINALLY, he straightened the antenna. "That should do it!" he said, and pressed the button with my name on it.

"Hercule!" I yelled. "What are you doing?"

Immediately, a swarm of BEEBOTS flew through the open factory door and headed right toward me. I closed my eyes, covered my snout with my paws, and prepared for the worst.

But all I felt were a few gentle bumps. Even the metallic *BUZZING* seemed softer. I opened one eye to see Hercule grinning in delight.

All done!

"It worked!" he cried. "I changed the software

so the bees won't attack you anymore. Now they want to be best friends."

I opened both eyes and saw that some of the **BEEBOTS** had landed on my head and shoulders.

"Hercule, you're a **genius**!" I cheered.

But just then Madame No came around the corner and spotted us.

"That's Geromino Stilton!" she cried. **"QUICK, STING HIM!"**

But the **BEEBOTS** still wouldn't try to **STING** me. Instead, they rose up in a **CLOUD** and moved back and forth in

formation — almost like they were saying "NO!"

Madame No jumped up and down in a RAGE. "Ungrateful bees! I created you. You have to do what I say!"

"Not anymore," Hercule said. "I reprogrammed them. Now they're free to do whatever they want."

Madame No **HOWLED** in anger.

STING HIM!

The BeeBots began to *BUZZ* loudly and fly closer to Madame No. She grabbed her **LEOPARD-PRINT** bag and swung it around, hitting some of the bees. "Listen to me! Sting Stilton!"

She kept yelling, but the BeeBots weren't listening. Suddenly, the *BUZZING* sounded angry, and Madame No's face turned as pale as fresh mozzarella.

"Professor!" she screamed. "Time to go!" She ran for her car and Professor No sprinted after her. "I've had enough of bees! Time to shut everything down!" they heard her yell as the leopard-print car zoomed out of the factory, Professor No hanging halfway out one of the doors.

Hercule cheered. The **BEEBOTS** buzzed happily.

"I guess we should take the **BEEBOTS**

back to the farm with us," I said. "There's nothing for them here now."

"To the **beecopter**!" Hercule shouted.

I frowned. "Maybe I'll just walk . . ."

"Don't be a worryrat, Geronimo! I'll go slowly this time, I promise!"

I groaned but followed Hercule back to the copter and climbed in.

"I can't believe Madame No was making fake honey this whole time. No wonder everymouse on the island had an upset **stomachache**. They were eating bad honey and getting sick," I said as the beecopter lifted into the air.

We passed over the TummyFix factory and I gasped. "Of course! Madame No must have also built the TummyFix factory right here. She was tricking rodents into buying fake honey so that they would get sick and she could sell them her **stomachache** cure!"

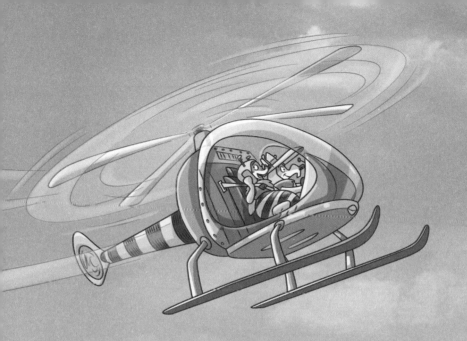

Hercule shook his snout. "Unbelievable," he said.

"Don't you mean, un-bee-lievable?" I said. I chuckled, but Hercule only rolled his eyes.

Now that I had cracked the **stomachache** case, I had to get an article ready for *The Rodent's Gazette*! The whole way back to the farm, I jotted down notes. I was so busy writing down my thoughts, I didn't even have time to get **airsick**!

# LONG LIVE STILTON FARM HONEY!

A week later, I was hosting a party at Stilton Farm to celebrate the success of the new honey business. I had even decided to wear my special bee suit again!

We were also celebrating the defeat of Madame No. With her fake honey off the market, our business was **BOOMING**. And *The Rodent's Gazette* article about Bee Mine had saved many rodents from getting sick on bad honey.

This was the last weekend of my **vacation**. I was sad I wouldn't be here every day, but I'd still be coming up as often as I could. Trap and I were going to take turns caring for the **beehives**, and Alpine and Melanie said they wanted to help out as well.

Grandfather William patted me on my back. "Well done, Grandson. *The Rodent's Gazette* published an impressive **scoop**!"

Just then, Trap called the rodents to attention by **banging** a spoon on a lid. "It's time for a picnic lunch!" he called. "I made three different kinds of **CHEESE**-and-**honey** desserts!"

While we had all been enjoying the party, Hercule had been repairing all the BeeBots. He was wearing his bee suit again, of course! Many of the BeeBots had wings, antennae, and stingers that needed **FIXING**. Madame No hadn't

*Well done, Grandson!*

been taking very good care of her ROBOTIC workers.

Hercule claimed he could even understand what they said when they buzzed. I wasn't so sure about that. But maybe he was right . . .

As I walked over to him, a group of BeeBots presented Hercule with a fresh flower garland. He happily put it around his neck. Then he listened, smiling as they *BUZZED* something in his ear.

"The BEEBOTS have a special request, Geronimo," he said. "They'd like to stay at Stilton Farm and help out with the honey."

I grinned. "Of course! All bees are welcome here!"

Hercule cheered and the BeeBots buzzed **happily**.

I think this is the **bee**-ginning of a very **bee**-utiful friendship!

# Don't miss a single fabumouse adventure!

## Up Next:

Don't miss any of my adventures in the Kingdom of Fantasy!

**THE KINGDOM OF FANTASY**

**THE QUEST FOR PARADISE:**
THE RETURN TO THE KINGDOM OF FANTASY

**THE AMAZING VOYAGE:**
THE THIRD ADVENTURE IN THE KINGDOM OF FANTASY

**THE DRAGON PROPHECY:**
THE FOURTH ADVENTURE IN THE KINGDOM OF FANTASY

**THE VOLCANO OF FIRE:**
THE FIFTH ADVENTURE IN THE KINGDOM OF FANTASY

**THE SEARCH FOR TREASURE:**
THE SIXTH ADVENTURE IN THE KINGDOM OF FANTASY

**THE ENCHANTED CHARMS:**
THE SEVENTH ADVENTURE IN THE KINGDOM OF FANTASY

**THE PHOENIX OF DESTINY:**
AN EPIC KINGDOM OF FANTASY ADVENTURE

**THE HOUR OF MAGIC:**
THE EIGHTH ADVENTURE IN THE KINGDOM OF FANTASY

**THE WIZARD'S WAND:**
THE NINTH ADVENTURE IN THE KINGDOM OF FANTASY

**THE SHIP OF SECRETS:**
THE TENTH ADVENTURE IN THE KINGDOM OF FANTASY

**THE DRAGON OF FORTUNE:**
AN EPIC KINGDOM OF FANTASY ADVENTURE

**THE GUARDIAN OF THE REALM:**
THE ELEVENTH ADVENTURE IN THE KINGDOM OF FANTASY

**THE ISLAND OF DRAGONS:**
THE TWELFTH ADVENTURE IN THE KINGDOM OF FANTASY

# Visit Geronimo in every universe!

## Spacemice

Geronimo Stiltonix and his crew are out of this world!

## Cavemice

Geronimo Stiltonoot, an ancient ancestor, is friends with the dinosaurs in the Stone Age!

## Micekings

Geronimo Stiltonord lives amongst the dragons in the ancient far north!

# Don't miss any of these exciting Thea Sisters adventures!

Thea Stilton and the
Dragon's Code

Thea Stilton and the
Mountain of Fire

Thea Stilton and the
Ghost of the Shipwreck

Thea Stilton and the
Secret City

Thea Stilton and the
Mystery in Paris

Thea Stilton and the
Cherry Blossom Adventure

Thea Stilton and the
Star Castaways

Thea Stilton: Big Trouble
in the Big Apple

Thea Stilton and the
Ice Treasure

Thea Stilton and the
Secret of the Old Castle

Thea Stilton and the
Blue Scarab Hunt

Thea Stilton and the
Prince's Emerald

Thea Stilton and the
Mystery on the Orient Express

Thea Stilton and the
Dancing Shadows

Thea Stilton and the
Legend of the Fire Flowers

Thea Stilton and the
Spanish Dance Mission

**Thea Stilton and the Journey to the Lion's Den**

**Thea Stilton and the Great Tulip Heist**

**Thea Stilton and the Chocolate Sabotage**

**Thea Stilton and the Missing Myth**

**Thea Stilton and the Lost Letters**

**Thea Stilton and the Tropical Treasure**

**Thea Stilton and the Hollywood Hoax**

**Thea Stilton and the Madagascar Madness**

**Thea Stilton and the Frozen Fiasco**

**Thea Stilton and the Venice Masquerade**

**Thea Stilton and the Niagara Splash**

**Thea Stilton and the Riddle of the Ruins**

**Thea Stilton and the Phantom of the Orchestra**

**Thea Stilton and the Black Forest Burglary**

**Thea Stilton and the Race for the Gold**

**Thea Stilton**

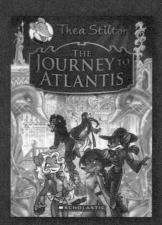

**Secret Fairies**

*Don't miss any of these exciting series featuring the Thea Sisters!*

**Treasure Seekers**

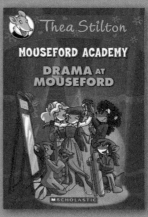

**Mouseford Academy**

1. Main entrance
2. Printing presses (where the books and newspaper are printed)
3. Accounts department
4. Editorial room (where the editors, illustrators, and designers work)
5. Geronimo Stilton's office
6. Helicopter landing pad

THE RODENT'S GAZETTE

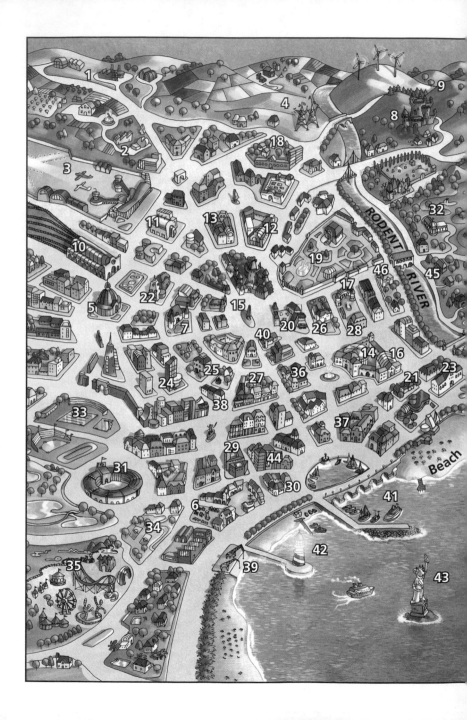

# Map of New Mouse City

# Map of Mouse Island

1. Big Ice Lake
2. Frozen Fur Peak
3. Slipperyslopes Glacier
4. Coldcreeps Peak
5. Ratzikistan
6. Transratania
7. Mount Vamp
8. Roastedrat Volcano
9. Brimstone Lake
10. Poopedcat Pass
11. Stinko Peak
12. Dark Forest
13. Vain Vampires Valley
14. Goose Bumps Gorge
15. The Shadow Line Pass
16. Penny Pincher Castle
17. Nature Reserve Park
18. Las Ratayas Marinas
19. Fossil Forest
20. Lake Lake
21. Lake Lakelake
22. Lake Lakelakelake
23. Cheddar Crag
24. Cannycat Castle
25. Valley of the Giant Sequoia
26. Cheddar Springs
27. Sulfurous Swamp
28. Old Reliable Geyser
29. Vole Vale
30. Ravingrat Ravine
31. Gnat Marshes
32. Munster Highlands
33. Mousehara Desert
34. Oasis of the Sweaty Camel
35. Cabbagehead Hill
36. Rattytrap Jungle
37. Rio Mosquito

Dear mouse friends,
Thanks for reading, and farewell
till the next book.
It'll be another whisker-licking-good
adventure, and that's a promise!

Geronimo